THE BOXCAR CHILDREN
SURPRISE ISLAND
THE YELLOW HOUSE MYSTERY
MYSTERY RANCH
MIKE'S MYSTERY
BLUE BAY MYSTERY
THE WOODSHED MYSTERY
THE LIGHTHOUSE MYSTERY
MOUNTAIN TOP MYSTERY
SCHOOLHOUSE MYSTERY
CABOOSE MYSTERY
HOUSEBOAT MYSTERY
SNOWBOUND MYSTERY
TREE HOUSE MYSTERY
BICYCLE MYSTERY
MYSTERY IN THE SAND
MYSTERY BEHIND THE WALL
BUS STATION MYSTERY
BENNY UNCOVERS A MYSTERY
THE HAUNTED CABIN MYSTERY
THE DESERTED LIBRARY MYSTERY
THE ANIMAL SHELTER MYSTERY
THE OLD MOTEL MYSTERY
THE MYSTERY OF THE HIDDEN PAINTING
THE AMUSEMENT PARK MYSTERY
THE MYSTERY OF THE MIXED-UP ZOO
THE CAMP-OUT MYSTERY
THE MYSTERY GIRL
THE MYSTERY CRUISE
THE DISAPPEARING FRIEND MYSTERY
THE MYSTERY OF THE SINGING GHOST
THE MYSTERY IN THE SNOW
THE PIZZA MYSTERY
THE MYSTERY HORSE
THE MYSTERY AT THE DOG SHOW
THE CASTLE MYSTERY
THE MYSTERY OF THE LOST VILLAGE
THE MYSTERY ON THE ICE
THE MYSTERY OF THE PURPLE POOL
THE GHOST SHIP MYSTERY
THE MYSTERY IN WASHINGTON, DC
THE CANOE TRIP MYSTERY

THE MYSTERY OF THE HIDDEN BEACH
THE MYSTERY OF THE MISSING CAT
THE MYSTERY AT SNOWFLAKE INN
THE MYSTERY ON STAGE
THE DINOSAUR MYSTERY
THE MYSTERY OF THE STOLEN MUSIC
THE MYSTERY AT THE BALL PARK
THE CHOCOLATE SUNDAE MYSTERY
THE MYSTERY OF THE HOT AIR BALLOON
THE MYSTERY BOOKSTORE
THE PILGRIM VILLAGE MYSTERY
THE MYSTERY OF THE STOLEN BOXCAR
THE MYSTERY IN THE CAVE
THE MYSTERY ON THE TRAIN
THE MYSTERY AT THE FAIR
THE MYSTERY OF THE LOST MINE
THE GUIDE DOG MYSTERY
THE HURRICANE MYSTERY
THE PET SHOP MYSTERY
THE MYSTERY OF THE SECRET MESSAGE
THE FIREHOUSE MYSTERY
THE MYSTERY IN SAN FRANCISCO
THE NIAGARA FALLS MYSTERY
THE MYSTERY AT THE ALAMO
THE OUTER SPACE MYSTERY
THE SOCCER MYSTERY
THE MYSTERY IN THE OLD ATTIC
THE GROWLING BEAR MYSTERY
THE MYSTERY OF THE LAKE MONSTER
THE MYSTERY AT PEACOCK HALL
THE WINDY CITY MYSTERY
THE BLACK PEARL MYSTERY
THE CEREAL BOX MYSTERY
THE PANTHER MYSTERY
THE MYSTERY OF THE QUEEN'S JEWELS
THE STOLEN SWORD MYSTERY
THE BASKETBALL MYSTERY
THE MOVIE STAR MYSTERY
THE MYSTERY OF THE PIRATE'S MAP
THE GHOST TOWN MYSTERY
THE MYSTERY OF THE BLACK RAVEN
THE MYSTERY IN THE MALL

The Mystery in New York
The Gymnastics Mystery
The Poison Frog Mystery
The Mystery of the Empty Safe
The Home Run Mystery
The Great Bicycle Race Mystery
The Mystery of the Wild Ponies
The Mystery in the Computer Game
The Honeybee Mystery
The Mystery at the Crooked House
The Hockey Mystery
The Mystery of the Midnight Dog
The Mystery of the Screech Owl
The Summer Camp Mystery
The Copycat Mystery
The Haunted Clock Tower Mystery
The Mystery of the Tiger's Eye
The Disappearing Staircase Mystery
The Mystery on Blizzard Mountain
The Mystery of the Spider's Clue
The Candy Factory Mystery
The Mystery of the Mummy's Curse
The Mystery of the Star Ruby
The Stuffed Bear Mystery
The Mystery of Alligator Swamp
The Mystery at Skeleton Point
The Tattletale Mystery
The Comic Book Mystery
The Great Shark Mystery
The Ice Cream Mystery
The Midnight Mystery
The Mystery in the Fortune Cookie
The Black Widow Spider Mystery
The Radio Mystery
The Mystery of the Runaway Ghost
The Finders Keepers Mystery
The Mystery of the Haunted Boxcar
The Clue in the Corn Maze
The Ghost of the Chattering Bones
The Sword of the Silver Knight
The Game Store Mystery
The Mystery of the Orphan Train
The Vanishing Passenger
The Giant Yo-Yo Mystery

The Creature in Ogopogo Lake
The Rock 'n' Roll Mystery
The Secret of the Mask
The Seattle Puzzle
The Ghost in the First Row
The Box That Watch Found
A Horse Named Dragon
The Great Detective Race
The Ghost at the Drive-In Movie
The Mystery of the Traveling Tomatoes
The Spy Game
The Dog-Gone Mystery
The Vampire Mystery
Superstar Watch
The Spy in the Bleachers
The Amazing Mystery Show
The Pumpkin Head Mystery
The Cupcake Caper
The Clue in the Recycling Bin
Monkey Trouble
The Zombie Project
The Great Turkey Heist
The Garden Thief
The Boardwalk Mystery
The Mystery of the Fallen Treasure
The Return of the Graveyard Ghost
The Mystery of the Stolen Snowboard
The Mystery of the Wild West Bandit
The Mystery of the Grinning Gargoyle
The Mystery of the Soccer Snitch
The Mystery of the Missing Pop Idol
The Mystery of the Stolen Dinosaur Bones
The Mystery at the Calgary Stampede
The Sleepy Hollow Mystery
The Legend of the Irish Castle
The Celebrity Cat Caper
Hidden in the Haunted School
The Election Day Dilemma
Journey on a Runaway Train
The Clue in the Papyrus Scroll
The Detour of the Elephants
The Shackleton Sabotage
The Khipu and the Final Key

THE MYSTERY AT THE CROOKED HOUSE

created by
GERTRUDE CHANDLER WARNER

Illustrated by Hodges Soileau

Albert Whitman & Company
Chicago, Illinois

Contents

THE MYSTERY AT THE CROOKED HOUSE

CHAPTER 1

The Marshmallow Mix-up

"Guess who's helping decorate the tree," said six-year-old Benny. Watch came running across the snowy backyard with a popcorn ball in his mouth. "Even Watch wants to help the birds!"

Twelve-year-old Jessie was hanging a string of cranberries from the branches of a pine tree. She turned and smiled at their little dog. "Watch knows it's hard for birds to find food in the winter."

"Everything is frozen and covered with snow at this time of year," added ten-year-

old Violet as she tightened the purple scarf around her neck. Purple was Violet's favorite color, and she almost always wore something purple or violet.

"Not all birds fly south," added Henry. He took the popcorn ball from Watch and hung it from one of the higher branches. At fourteen, Henry was the oldest of the Alden children. "Some birds stay where it's cold. They make their homes wherever they can find a warm, dry spot."

Benny glanced over his shoulder at their red boxcar. "Just like we did!"

He was thinking back to when they had discovered the old abandoned train car in the woods. Their parents had died, and they were hiding from their grandfather because they thought he was mean. But Grandfather Alden wasn't mean at all.

After finding his grandchildren, Grandfather Alden had brought the four Aldens and Watch to live with him in his big white house on the edge of the town of Greenfield, Connecticut. And when he had realized how much they missed the boxcar,

Grandfather Alden had given their old home a special place in his backyard. Now the Aldens often used the boxcar as a clubhouse.

Jessie stepped back to admire their tree. She clapped her mittened hands together and said, "What a feast the birds will have!"

Violet went over and stood beside her older sister. The tree was quite a sight, with its decorations of popcorn balls, apple rings, loops of red cranberries and unshelled peanuts, corn on the cob, and little mesh bags of suet. Everything was tied to the branches with brightly colored yarn.

"Birds have huge appetites," Violet said softly. "Even a tiny hummingbird eats every ten minutes or so!"

Benny grinned. "No wonder they hum. They must be very happy birds!"

They all laughed. The youngest Alden was *always* hungry.

"I'll bet we'll soon have lots of visitors," remarked Henry.

Benny was stomping his feet to keep

them warm. He had a look of concern on his face. "But what if the birds don't spot our tree?"

"Don't worry, Benny," said Violet. "The chickadees will find it. Other birds hang around chickadees because they're such good food-finders!"

"Just like we're good clue-finders!" said Benny. And his brother and sisters nodded in agreement. The Aldens loved mysteries, and together they'd managed to solve quite a few. "But are you *sure* the chickadees will find our tree?" Benny asked.

"Maybe we should leave an invitation for them!" suggested Henry, hiding a smile. He knelt down and began to write in the snow. When he was finished, he got up and brushed the snow from his pant legs.

"I know what *that* says!" Benny announced proudly. The youngest Alden always enjoyed a chance to show his older brother and sisters that he was learning how to read. "It says, '*Welcome Birds!*' "

Violet stooped down and added something to Henry's invitation. "*And . . . bring . . . all . . . your . . . friends!*"

"That should *really* do the trick!" said Benny.

Jessie was staring down at the writing in the snow. "A person's handwriting is supposed to show some interesting things," she said.

"Like what?" asked Violet.

"Well, Henry's handwriting slants to the right a bit," said Jessie, who had been reading a book on handwriting. "That's supposed to show he's a very friendly person. And he's careful with each letter. I can tell he's probably a hard worker, too."

"Jessie's right, Henry!" said Violet. "You *are* a hard worker. And you're always friendly to everyone!"

Henry looked pleased. "What about Violet's handwriting?" he asked.

"Hmmm." Jessie took another look. "Well, I can see some fancy swirls. That's a sign of a person who's artistic . . . and helpful, too," Jessie concluded.

"You *do* like to draw pictures, Violet," observed Benny. "And you're good at it!" he added.

Just then the back door of the house opened. Mrs. McGregor came out carrying a tray. There were four cups of steaming hot chocolate and a plate of chocolate chip cookies on it.

"Oh, boy!" cried Benny. "How did you know I was hungry, Mrs. McGregor?"

Mrs. McGregor broke into a smile as she came along the shoveled walkway. "Just a hunch, Benny." She set the tray down on the tree stump that was the boxcar's front step. "Besides," she added, "what could be better on a cold winter's day than hot chocolate with marshmallows?"

Benny reached out for his special cup. It was the cracked pink cup he had found when they were living in the boxcar. "I love hot chocolate with marshmallows in it!" he said. But when he looked down, he gasped in surprise.

"What is it?" asked Jessie, who often acted like a mother to her younger brother and sister. "What's wrong, Benny?"

"The . . . the marshmallows!" cried Benny. "These are the funniest-looking marshmallows I ever saw!"

"Why, whatever do you mean?" asked Mrs. McGregor.

"Well, they look just like mushrooms!" said Benny.

And sure enough, mushrooms were floating in their hot chocolate!

"Oh — oh, my!" cried Mrs. McGregor. "How could I have made such a mistake?" Then she slapped a hand against her cheek. "Don't tell me . . . Oh, my goodness! I must have put the marshmallows in the stew!" And with that, Mrs. McGregor rushed back to the house.

The Alden children stared after her in amazement. Henry was shaking his head. "That's not like Mrs. McGregor," he said.

"No, it's not," agreed Jessie. "But she hasn't been acting like herself at all lately. I spoke to her twice today and she didn't answer. She seemed to be deep in thought."

"Mrs. McGregor must be worried about something," said Violet. "I think we should find out what's wrong. Maybe we can help."

"Well, what are we waiting for?" cried Benny. Forgetting all about food, he went racing along the walkway with his brother and sisters close behind.

Whatever was wrong with Mrs. Mc-Gregor, the Aldens were determined to set it right!

CHAPTER 2

The Crooked House
at Riddle Lake

After hanging their jackets on the coat tree by the door, the Aldens struggled out of their boots and went looking for Mrs. McGregor. They found her in the living room. She was sitting in the green satin chair by the window. At her feet was a wicker basket filled with their old clothes.

"Oh, dear!" she said as Henry, Jessie, Violet, and Benny came into the room. "I meant to make another pot of hot chocolate for you."

"That's okay, Mrs. McGregor," said

Henry as he sat down on the couch. "We didn't come in for hot chocolate."

Mrs. McGregor went back to her work. She was making a braided rag rug. For the last week, she had been tearing their old clothing into long, thin strips, which she braided together. Then she wrapped the braids around and around and stitched them in place to form a circle.

"What a great way to recycle our old clothes!" said Violet, who was standing by Mrs. McGregor's chair. "It's fun watching the circle grow bigger every day."

"And it has every color of the rainbow in it," said Jessie. "Watch will love it."

Mrs. McGregor smiled. "The rug will have something from each of the Alden children in it," she said. "What could be better than that?"

Benny was warming his hands by the fire. "Maybe when it's finished, we can put the braided rag rug in the boxcar."

"Yes," agreed Violet. "That'll be just the place for it! Don't you think so, Mrs. McGregor?"

But Mrs. McGregor made no reply. Her head was bent over her work and she seemed to be lost in a world of her own. Jessie looked over at Henry as if to say, *Now, this is exactly what I was talking about!*

Violet reached out and put a hand gently on their housekeeper's arm. "Mrs. McGregor?" she said. "Is anything wrong?"

"Oh, I'm sorry, Violet," said Mrs. McGregor. "I wasn't listening. What were you saying?"

"Please, Mrs. McGregor," pleaded Violet, "won't you tell us what's troubling you?"

"Sometimes talking about a problem can help," added Jessie.

Just then, Watch came over and put his head in Mrs. McGregor's lap. He gave a little whimper. "Look!" cried Benny. "Even Watch is worried!"

"Oh, dear!" Mrs. McGregor scratched Watch behind the ears. "I really didn't mean to cause such a fuss! The truth is," she added, "something has been bothering me. But I'm afraid there's nothing anyone can do to help."

"But haven't you seen Violet's swirls? Jessie says the swirls mean she's helpful," cried Benny. "We *all* can be *very* helpful!"

"Oh, Benny!" Jessie laughed. "Violet would be helpful even if her handwriting didn't have a single swirl in it!"

Mrs. McGregor was quiet for a moment, then she said, "I've been racking my brains trying to come up with an answer to a problem. I'm afraid the Crooked House has been on my mind all day."

Benny glanced around. "But Grandfather's house isn't crooked!"

Mrs. McGregor shook her head. "I mean the Crooked House at Riddle Lake."

The Aldens stared at Mrs. McGregor in bewilderment. They had never heard of a Crooked House at Riddle Lake.

"It's my family home," explained Mrs. McGregor. "My father built it himself, and everything turned out just a little bit crooked. You see, my father had never built anything before then."

"I'll bet he had fun, though," said Henry, who liked building things.

"I think my father really *did* enjoy building our home," Mrs. McGregor continued. "And we loved all the crooked windows and the crooked doors — and the floor that was on a bit of a slant." Mrs. McGregor paused for a moment. "My sister Madeline and I inherited the family home after our parents died. That was many years ago. At first, Madeline wanted to sell the Crooked House so she could do a bit of traveling. When we were growing up, she'd always talked of seeing the world. But the truth is, neither of us could bear to part with our family home."

Mrs. McGregor went on, "Madeline continued living there instead. And she's been making a very comfortable living all these years, renting out rooms to folks from the city. Just like our parents did. Riddle Lake really is a wonderful place for a holiday. There's swimming and hiking and fishing in the summer. And skating and tobogganing and cross-country skiing in the winter."

"Wow!" said Henry. "That sure sounds great!"

Mrs. McGregor let out another long sigh. "Yes, but I'm afraid things haven't been going very well lately at the Crooked House."

"Why not?" asked Violet in surprise.

"Last year a fancy resort was built at the other end of Riddle Lake," explained Mrs. McGregor. "Now people seem to prefer the modern Sterling Resort to the old-fashioned comforts of the Crooked House. I'm afraid business has fallen off. My sister says there isn't enough money to pay the taxes this year.

"Madeline phoned this morning and asked me to drive up to Riddle Lake for a few days. She thinks it's time we made a decision about selling the family home. It'll break our hearts, but there doesn't seem to be any other choice." Mrs. McGregor's eyes clouded. "I'll leave tomorrow. There's no point in delaying what must be done. Besides, I haven't seen Madeline for a while. Not since we made that trip to Oregon together."

Just then a rush of cold air stirred the curtains on the window as Grandfather

Alden came through the door. He stopped in his tracks when he saw the long faces. "What's this all about?" he asked with concern. When everybody began to speak at once, he held up his hands. "Whoa!" he said. "One at a time!"

Taking turns, they told their grandfather all about the Crooked House at Riddle Lake. Then Mrs. McGregor said, "I haven't had my mind on my work today. I'm afraid dinner is ruined."

"I have an idea," said Grandfather Alden after a moment's thought. "Why don't we go to Joe's Restaurant for pizza?"

"Mmmm!" said Benny. "An extra-large pizza with everything on it?"

Everyone laughed. They laughed even harder when Mrs. McGregor said, "Maybe everything except mushrooms, Benny!"

CHAPTER 3

Hold the Mushrooms!

"Well," said Grandfather Alden, patting his stomach, "I couldn't eat another bite if you paid me!" They were sitting in a booth at Joe's Restaurant.

"Nor could I!" agreed Mrs. McGregor.

"I think I have room for more," Benny piped up. There was one slice of pizza left. It was Benny's favorite kind — topped with special tomato sauce, extra cheese, and pepperoni. "Unless somebody else wants it," he added politely.

Jessie shook her head. "Go ahead, Benny," she said. "I'm stuffed!"

Benny used both hands to pick up the pizza. "I eat like a bird!" he said. Then he added with a grin, "But just remember, even a hummingbird eats every ten minutes!"

Everyone laughed at Benny's joke. Then Mrs. McGregor took a sip of her tea. "That pizza really *did* hit the spot. And not a single mushroom in sight!" she said with a laugh.

"It's good to see you in better spirits, Mrs. McGregor," Grandfather said.

"How could anyone *not* be in good spirits around the Aldens? But I really must leave for Riddle Lake tomorrow," Mrs. McGregor added as she grew serious again. "Oh, dear! I really will miss my family home when it's sold!"

"We missed our old home, too," admitted Jessie, "until Grandfather surprised us one day!"

The Alden children looked gratefully at their grandfather, remembering the day he had moved the boxcar all the way from the woods to the backyard of their Greenfield home.

Mrs. McGregor nodded. "Any place that has been a home will always be very dear to the heart," she said. "But I'm afraid my sister is right. We just can't afford to keep the Crooked House now that the resort has opened."

Grandfather was thumping a finger against his chin. He put down his coffee cup and said, "It seems to me that if you were to advertise, business just might pick up. I'm sure there are plenty of people who would prefer the peace and quiet of the Crooked House to the hustle and bustle of a big resort."

Henry, Jessie, Violet, and Benny all leaned forward when their grandfather spoke. James Alden knew all there was to know about business.

"Yes," agreed Mrs. McGregor. "Advertising would help. But it takes money to advertise. And money is the one thing we don't have."

"If I knew what the Crooked House looked like," Violet said in her gentle voice, "I'd draw a picture of it for you, Mrs. McGregor. Then you could see it whenever you wanted."

Mrs. McGregor drew in her breath as a sudden thought came to her. "Why don't you come along?" she suggested. Then, turning to James Alden, she added, "Do you think you could spare your grandchildren for a few days? I know they'd have a wonderful time at Riddle Lake."

"We would miss you, Grandfather," said Jessie, "but we *would* like to see Mrs. McGregor's family home!"

"May we go, Grandfather?" asked Violet. "Then I really could draw that picture for Mrs. McGregor!"

"Plus there's tobogganing!" Benny managed to say as he took the last bite of his pizza.

"And skating!" added Henry, who sounded very excited.

"Well, now," said Grandfather Alden, his eyes twinkling, "perhaps I could make do

on my own for a few days — if Watch stays behind and keeps me company."

"Hooray!" cried Benny. "Riddle Lake, here we come!"

"As a matter of fact," Grandfather went on, "I have business not far from there. I'd be happy to drive you up to Riddle Lake tomorrow. That is, if you don't mind leaving after lunch. I'm afraid I have a meeting to attend in the morning."

"That's very kind of you." Mrs. McGregor sounded very pleased.

"I've been wondering about something," said Jessie. "Why do they call it *Riddle* Lake?"

"Nobody knows how the lake got its name," replied Mrs. McGregor. "I suppose that's a riddle in itself."

"And a riddle is a kind of question, isn't it?" asked Benny.

"Yes, it is!" said Mrs. McGregor. "You find the answer by trying to figure out the clues."

"Just like a mystery!" observed Violet.

"Right!" agreed Mrs. McGregor. "A riddle is exactly like a mystery."

"I know a riddle!" piped up Benny.

Grandfather laughed. "Tell us, Benny! I like a good riddle."

"What's black and white and red all over?"

"That's easy," said Henry. "The answer is a newspaper! It's black and white — and it gets *read* all over!"

Benny shook his head. "Nope! The answer is a sunburned zebra!"

Everybody laughed. Then Mrs. McGregor said, "When we get to the Crooked House, I will tell you a riddle that I have never been able to solve! When I was your age, I spent hours and hours trying to guess the answer."

"Won't you tell us now?" pleaded Benny.

Mrs. McGregor laughed. "I'll tell you when we get to the Crooked House," she promised. Then she added in a hushed voice, "But I will say this much: The answer is supposed to lead to a hidden treasure!"

The Alden children were staring wide-eyed at their housekeeper. The thought of a mystery waiting to be solved had them very excited.

How could anyone sell a house with a treasure inside? thought Violet.

Once again the Aldens were about to embark on an adventure!

CHAPTER 4

The Unfriendly Guest

On their way to the Crooked House the next day, Benny suddenly cried out, "Oh, no! I forgot to bring it." And he gave his forehead a smack with the palm of his hand.

"Bring what, Benny?" asked Jessie. She was sure he had packed all of his warm winter clothes and his cracked pink cup.

"The mystery book I got for Christmas!" said Benny. "The one by Amelia Quigley Adams. And we were just getting to the best part, Jessie!"

"Oh, *The Alphabet Mystery*!" Jessie had been reading a chapter every night to her brother. "I meant to pack it, but I guess I forgot, too."

"Don't worry, Benny," said Henry. "When Mrs. McGregor tells us the riddle, we'll have our own mystery to solve."

Violet put an arm around her younger brother. "And a treasure to find!" she added.

Mrs. McGregor was sitting up front beside Grandfather Alden. She looked over her shoulder and said, "You're in luck, Benny! Amelia Quigley Adams was my favorite children's author when I was growing up. There's a whole collection of her books at the Crooked House. In fact, I have a signed copy of *The Alphabet Mystery*."

Benny's round face brightened. "Hooray for the Crooked House!"

At that moment, they passed a huge billboard advertisement for the Sterling Resort. Mrs. McGregor shook her head. "With advertising like that, the Crooked House doesn't stand a chance."

As they turned off the main highway and

drove along the lake, they caught a glimpse of the new resort through the trees. Mrs. McGregor went on, "Of course, a few people have remained loyal to the Crooked House. They still come out for their holidays. But my sister has always relied on new guests as well."

Snowflakes were just starting to drift down when they came to a small sign advertising rooms to rent. The sign was nailed to a crooked post. The Aldens' station wagon turned into a long driveway piled high with snow on either side. At the end of the driveway was a big, old-fashioned cottage nestled among the trees. An evergreen wreath decorated its crooked front door.

As Jessie got out of the car, she noticed a man in a hooded black coat shoveling snow in the next driveway. A young girl wearing a blue ski jacket was helping him.

"Those windows really *are* lopsided!" said Henry as he opened the car door for Mrs. McGregor.

"Oh, yes," said Mrs. McGregor, gazing fondly at her family home. "There isn't a single window that's straight. Some go this way and some go that!"

"And look!" cried Benny, pointing. "The chimney's crooked, too! It looks like that funny tower. The one that leans over."

Grandfather Alden chuckled as he lifted the suitcases out of the car. "I think you mean the Leaning Tower of Pisa, Benny."

"Right." Benny nodded. "The Leaning Tower of Pisa in, um . . ."

"Italy," finished Jessie.

"Never fear, Benny," said Mrs. McGregor. "There's no danger of the crooked chimney tumbling over. It always passes inspection."

"What a wonderful home, Mrs. McGregor," Violet said in a soft voice. "I can't wait to draw a picture of it for you."

Their housekeeper was beaming proudly. "The property backs right onto the lake. You won't have far to go for skating."

Just then the front door of the Crooked

House opened. A white-haired woman waved out to them. She looked a lot like Mrs. McGregor, only taller.

Mrs. McGregor waved back. "That's my sister, Madeline!"

The man in the next driveway tossed his shovel aside, then the young girl tossed hers aside, too, and they came rushing over.

"I'm Nick Spencer." The man pushed the hood of his coat back from his dark curly hair. "And this is my daughter, Clarissa."

"We live just next door," said Clarissa with a dimpled smile. She was about Violet's age and was wearing a knit hat that matched her jacket. The breeze kept stirring the wisps of blond curls that framed her rosy face.

"James Alden," said Grandfather, putting a hand out to Nick. "And this is Mrs. McGregor and my grandchildren: Henry, Jessie, Violet, and Benny."

"I must tell you, Mrs. McGregor," said Nick, "we're really going to miss your sister if the Crooked House is sold. We'll never be able to repay her for all her kind-

ness. She's been like a grandmother to Clarissa and a good friend to me."

Mrs. McGregor smiled. "My sister has always spoken highly of you, too. You teach history at the local high school, don't you, Nick?"

Nick nodded and smiled. "History has always fascinated me. There's something so mysterious about the past. You never know what treasures you'll uncover when you start poking about."

Jessie and Henry exchanged looks. Was it just a coincidence that Nick had used the word *treasure*?

Nick and Clarissa helped Mrs. McGregor with her bags as they all trooped along a path through the snow, then stepped into a hallway cheerfully decorated with sprigs of evergreen and holly. While they breathed in the wonderful smell of home cooking, Mrs. McGregor gave her sister a warm hug. Then she introduced the Aldens.

"Welcome to the Crooked House!" said Madeline. "You must be hungry after that long drive. Will you and Clarissa join us for dinner, Nick?" she added. "You know there's always plenty to go around."

But Nick and Clarissa were already on their way out the door. "Thanks anyway, Madeline," said Nick. "We'll have to take a rain check. We've got the driveway to finish, then we're off to the library." With a wave of his hand, he added, "Sure nice to meet everybody, though!"

Grandfather looked at his watch. "I'm afraid I'd better be going, too. I still have some business to take care of."

"Grandfather doesn't like to keep anyone waiting," said Henry.

The children stood at the door and waved good-bye until the station wagon disappeared behind the trees. Then they took off their coats and boots and hung their knit hats on the hat tree by the door. After that, it wasn't long before they were sitting down to a delicious dinner of meat loaf, baked potatoes, tossed salad, and creamed corn.

"Mmm," said Benny. "This meat loaf tastes just like Mrs. McGregor's!"

"I got the recipe from Madeline," said

Mrs. McGregor as she buttered a crusty roll. "My sister is the *real* cook in the family."

"Nonsense!" argued Madeline. "You're every bit the cook I am, Margaret."

Benny's eyes widened. "I think I'm going to like it here!"

"That's for sure!" said Henry. "Two great cooks under one roof! That's a dream come true for you, Benny."

Jessie noticed there was an extra place at the table. She was just wondering about it when Madeline said, "We have a guest staying upstairs."

Mrs. McGregor raised her eyebrows in surprise. "Oh?"

Madeline nodded. "Yes, a young woman arrived the other day. Nola Rawlings. She's staying in the blue room at the end of the hall."

Mrs. McGregor looked hopeful. "Do you think business is improving?"

"Oh, I used to get my hopes up," said Madeline with a sigh. "But I've been disappointed too many times. I know better now."

Mrs. McGregor nodded. "I suppose you're right. A guest every now and again isn't enough."

Just then a slim young woman with shoulder-length brownish-red hair came into the room. She was dressed in jeans and a gray sweater.

Madeline rose to greet her, then quickly introduced Mrs. McGregor and the Aldens. Nola Rawlings responded with a brisk nod as she slipped into the empty chair beside Henry.

Mrs. McGregor smiled warmly. "Are you enjoying your stay at Riddle Lake, Nola?"

The young woman didn't answer right away. She placed a napkin carefully over her lap, then she looked over at the Aldens with a frown. "I've enjoyed it so far," she finally said. "I came to Riddle Lake *hoping* to find peace and quiet."

The children exchanged puzzled glances. Why was Nola so unfriendly?

Mrs. McGregor tried to change the subject. "By the way, Benny, that book you want is on a shelf in the living room. Isn't it amazing about those mysteries by Amelia Quigley Adams? They're just as popular now as they were in my day! Did you read them when you were growing up, Nola?" she added.

The young woman gave Mrs. McGregor a funny look. "Why do you ask?" she replied rather sharply.

"No reason, really," said Mrs. McGregor in surprise. "I just wondered if you were a fan of Amelia Quigley Adams. When I was growing up —"

Nola broke in before Mrs. McGregor could finish. "I've heard of her, of course. But I've never read any of her books. Nor do I have any interest in the subject!"

Everyone seemed surprised by the young woman's harsh tone. Jessie caught Henry's eye. It was such a simple question. Why was Nola getting so upset?

When dessert was served, Madeline commented, "It's nice to have so many people gathered around the table again. I'm just sorry that Nick and Clarissa couldn't join us."

"We're looking forward to getting to know Clarissa better," said Jessie, taking a bite of the delicious apple pie.

"Oh, you're bound to run into her when you go out skating," replied Madeline. "And just wait till you see the fancy twirls she can do!"

"Jessie is a good skater, too," Violet said shyly, looking at her older sister with admiration.

"I've still got a lot to learn," Jessie protested. "But I *do* enjoy it. I can't wait to get out there."

"Well, it's a beautiful night for it," said Madeline. "No reason you can't go right after dinner."

"There's a very *good* reason we can't go right after supper," Benny stated firmly. "Mrs. McGregor's going to tell us all about the riddle and the hidden treasure!"

The Aldens all nodded their agreement. Nobody noticed Madeline's sudden frown. Or the look of shock on Nola Rawlings's face.

CHAPTER 5

The Mystery Lady

After the Aldens helped with the dishes, they carried their suitcases up the crooked staircase behind Mrs. Mc-Gregor.

"Will you tell us about the riddle now?" Benny asked her.

"I won't keep you in suspense much longer," promised Mrs. McGregor. "As soon as you unpack, we'll have some cake by the fire. Then I'll tell you all about it."

Upstairs, Mrs. McGregor opened a door to a cozy room with cornflower-blue wallpaper and lace curtains. It was perfect for Jessie and Violet. And it was right across the hall from Henry and Benny's sunny yellow bedroom. Both rooms were furnished with twin beds covered in old-fashioned patchwork quilts and tall pine dressers with brass handles. There were also antique desks and ladderback chairs with crooked slats.

Violet especially liked the painting of Riddle Lake that was hanging in their room. It was a winter scene — with lots of snow and with icicles glistening on the trees. The painting looked just like the view from their window!

It didn't take the Aldens long to unpack. They were waiting for Violet to put away her sketchbook and pencils when Madeline passed the door. She paused in the hallway and said, "I certainly hope you'll enjoy your stay at the Crooked House!"

Jessie spoke for them all. "Oh, I'm sure we will!"

Madeline frowned. "I'm sure you'll enjoy it, too . . . as long as you forget all about that riddle! Believe me, you'll be wasting your time if you don't. Even if there *is* a treasure, which I doubt, it's probably nothing more than a rare coin or an old toy. If you think it's something of value, you'll just be getting your hopes up for nothing!"

The Aldens were too surprised to speak. Without saying another word, Madeline turned and hurried off toward the crooked staircase.

"I wonder why Madeline seems so upset," said Violet, looking puzzled.

Jessie frowned. "It *does* seem odd."

Benny sighed. He had been looking forward to finding a *real* treasure. Something worth a fortune. Or at least worth enough to save the Crooked House. "An old toy isn't much of a treasure," he said, disappointment in his voice.

"No, it's not," agreed Jessie. "And Madeline's not even sure there *is* a treasure!"

"But there might be," said Henry after a moment's thought. "And it *might* be valuable."

"That's true," said Jessie.

"So what do we do now?" asked Violet.

"Find out more!" suggested Benny, who always got right to the point. "And don't forget, Mrs. McGregor said something about cake!"

While Madeline went next door with some leftover meat loaf for Nick and Clarissa, the Aldens sat around the cozy fireplace in the living room. It was dark outside and the snow was still falling. But inside, the fire crackled cheerfully, and the spicy scent of pine filled the air.

Mrs. McGregor was sipping eggnog. The Alden children had asked her about the riddle and were waiting for her reply. When she finally spoke, her voice was almost a whisper. "It was the Mystery Lady who sent me the riddle," she said. "Many, many years ago."

Benny almost choked on his cake. "The Mystery Lady?"

Mrs. McGregor nodded. "I remember

her so well. Her hair was as white as the snow, but her heart was as warm as the fire. She rented a room every summer when I was a child. Oh, she always registered as Miss Jane Smith, but it wasn't long before we realized that Jane Smith wasn't her *real* name. You see, it always took her a moment to react when someone called her Miss Smith. We soon figured out that she just wasn't used to being called by that name. She never talked about her life away from Riddle Lake, you know. Not a single word."

Henry put his empty glass on the coffee table. "Is that why you called her the Mystery Lady?"

"Exactly," replied Mrs. McGregor. "I suppose it might seem odd that we would welcome an imposter into our home. But she was so gracious and kind. After a while, it just didn't matter who she really was. We called her the Mystery Lady, and she seemed to enjoy it." Mrs. McGregor had a faraway look in her eyes. "The Mystery Lady loved Riddle Lake. She even painted a picture of how she imagined it would look in the winter. She was only a beginner, but the painting is quite lovely. As a matter of fact, that painting's still hanging in her old room at the top of the stairs — the room that looks out onto the lake."

"Oh!" said Violet in surprise. "That painting's in the room Jessie and I are sharing!"

Mrs. McGregor gave a little nod and smiled. "She liked the view from that room. Actually, the lake was the reason the Mystery Lady and I became such good friends. I remember we had a long discussion one day about how it came to be called Riddle Lake. Of course, that's a mystery no one will ever solve. But that day, we realized we shared a common interest in riddles. Madeline always kept her distance, but the Mystery Lady and I soon became the best of friends!"

"Why did Madeline keep her distance?" asked Jessie curiously.

Mrs. McGregor sighed. "My sister likes everything to be out in the open. She's always been rather suspicious of anyone who has a . . . a hint of mystery about them. And our guest from long ago had far more than just a *hint* of mystery about her!"

"Did she ever tell you her *real* name?" asked Benny, his eyes round.

Mrs. McGregor shook her head. "No, we never discovered her true identity. It remains a secret to this very day. I guess I was always hoping that one day she'd tell me about her life away from Riddle Lake. But it never happened." A shadow seemed to pass over Mrs. McGregor's face. "One summer, the Mystery Lady suddenly just stopped coming to the Crooked House."

The Aldens were surprised to hear this. "You never heard from her again?" inquired Henry.

"She *never* got in touch?" asked Jessie at the same time.

"Just once, the winter after her last visit," said Mrs. McGregor. "I received a short note in the mail from the Mystery Lady. A note with a riddle and a promise that the answer would lead to a hidden treasure!"

Benny was jiggling up and down. "What was it, Mrs. McGregor? What was the riddle?"

Smiling at the youngest Alden's enthusiasm, Mrs. McGregor went over to a cupboard with glass doors. She took out a battered old shoe box and came back to her chair by the fire. Lifting the lid of the box, she fished out a folded piece of paper, yellowed with age.

As the Aldens leaned forward to catch every word, Mrs. McGregor unfolded the note and read the riddle aloud.

" 'What is the thing that
You never need fear
Though teeth like a dragon
It grows every year?
You'll find that its bark
Is much worse than its bite,
Though its dragonly teeth
Are a most scary sight!' "

"Teeth like a dragon?" echoed Benny in amazement.

Mrs. McGregor nodded. "There's also a
P.S. at the bottom of the note. It says, 'It
will take a second to uncover a hidden treasure.' And then it's signed 'The Mystery
Lady.'"

After hearing the riddle one more time,
Henry said, "That's a tough one!"

"Yes, indeed!" agreed Mrs. McGregor.
"And it certainly didn't take me a second to
uncover the hidden treasure! My goodness,
I must have spent hours and hours trying to
figure it out. Finally, I searched the house
from top to bottom. I was hoping I just
might come across the treasure that way."

Benny looked puzzled. "I wonder what
grows dragon teeth every year."

"Something that won't do any harm!" Violet reminded her younger brother.

"That's right." Henry nodded. "The riddle says its bark is worse than its bite."

Benny shoved the last few crumbs of cake
into his mouth. "That's just like our dog,
Watch! His bark is worse than his bite."

"That's because Watch doesn't bite at
all!" said Jessie, and everyone laughed.

Mrs. McGregor folded the note again. "I think teamwork is needed to answer this riddle and uncover the treasure. If anyone can do it, the Aldens can!"

"But Mrs. McGregor," Benny said doubtfully, "are you sure there *is* a treasure?"

"Oh, yes!" declared Mrs. McGregor. "I'm quite certain of it!"

Benny still looked worried. "But . . . what if it's just a coin or an old toy?"

Mrs. McGregor stared into the fire again. "I've always had a feeling the treasure had great importance to the Mystery Lady. But even a rare coin or an old toy would be special to me because it came from the Mystery Lady. When the Crooked House is sold, I'll always wonder what she left behind."

"I know what you mean," Jessie said thoughtfully. "We'll try very hard to find the treasure, Mrs. McGregor. Whatever it is!"

"We promise to do our best!" added Violet.

Mrs. McGregor smiled. "No one can ask more than that!"

Jessie thought of something. "Mrs. McGregor, do you mind if I make a copy of the riddle? That way we can take a quick look at it whenever we want, and the note can be tucked safely away."

"Good thinking!" said Henry, and Violet nodded. They could always count on Jessie to be organized.

Mrs. McGregor took a small pad of paper and a pen from her purse. She handed it to Jessie, along with the note. With her head bent, Jessie set to work copying the riddle by the light of the fire.

Nobody said anything for a moment, then Henry asked, "Mrs. McGregor, are there any photographs of the Mystery Lady?"

Mrs. McGregor began rummaging through the shoe box. "She never liked having her picture taken, but . . . I think there is *one* snapshot. Not an especially good one. Her face is hidden under a big straw hat."

Finally, Mrs. McGregor let out her breath. "Well, it's not here. But it must be around somewhere. I'll take a good look tomorrow."

When Jessie had finished scribbling out the riddle, she commented, "The Mystery Lady's handwriting has very high loops."

Mrs. McGregor looked surprised. "I guess I never noticed."

Jessie said, "That's usually a sign of someone who has a good imagination."

Mrs. McGregor broke into a wide smile. "Yes, the Mystery Lady had a wonderful imagination! We would often sit for hours under a tree. Oh, she would make up the most wonderful stories to entertain me!"

"I think Grandfather was right," said Henry as Mrs. McGregor put the yellowed note safely away in the shoe box. "We *will* need our wits about us to solve *this* riddle!"

"Please enjoy yourselves, too, while you're here," urged Mrs. McGregor. "I wouldn't want you to spend all your time trying to find the treasure. After all, there'll be a fresh blanket of snow for tobogganing tomorrow!"

Benny shot to his feet. "I wonder if it's still snowing."

As everyone rushed over to the window, Violet thought she caught a glimpse of movement in the hall. Was it just the flickering shadows of the fire? Or had someone been eavesdropping?

CHAPTER 6

Who in the World Is Rebecca Flagg?

Benny held out his cracked pink cup while Violet poured hot chocolate from a big thermos. "This'll sure warm me up!" he said.

The Aldens were sitting together on a snowy bank by the lake after a busy morning. Their day had started with a hearty breakfast of scrambled eggs, crispy bacon, toast, and pancakes with maple syrup. After breakfast, they had shoveled the snow from the long driveway. Then they'd carried the shovels down to the lake to clear a patch of ice for skating. Now they were taking a break from a friendly game of hockey.

"If something grows dragon teeth every year," Jessie was saying, "then it only makes sense that it must *lose* them every year, too."

"That's true," stated Violet. "But what loses its teeth every year and then grows new ones?"

Jessie shrugged as she pulled the riddle from her back pocket and read it again.

"That was a good idea to make a copy of the riddle, Jessie," said Violet, shoving the thermos back into her duffel bag.

Jessie nodded. "This way Mrs. McGregor can keep her note safe in the old shoe box."

"What I can't figure out," said Henry, "is why the Mystery Lady said it would take a *second* to find the treasure."

Benny looked discouraged. "It's taking us forever! How are we going to find the treasure if we can't answer the riddle? And we promised Mrs. McGregor!"

Henry put an arm around his younger brother. "We promised we'd do our best.

And we *will* do our best. We haven't given up yet, have we?"

"No!" the other Aldens shouted all together.

Nobody said anything for a while as they sipped their chocolate and enjoyed the peace and quiet. Finally, Jessie spoke up. "No wonder Mrs. McGregor wanted to visit her family home one more time. It's so beautiful up here at Riddle Lake."

"I wish I'd brought my camera!" said Violet. "Just look at how the icicles glisten on the trees! It's just like the Mystery Lady's painting." Violet had been admiring the painting again before she'd gone to bed.

"How can Nola be so grumpy," wondered Benny, "when she's staying in such a nice place?"

"She was just as unfriendly at breakfast," added Henry. "I wonder what's bothering her."

Just then the Aldens heard the creaking of boots on snow. They all turned quickly in surprise. Clarissa was standing behind them

with her skates slung over her shoulder.

"Hi, Clarissa!" Jessie called out with a friendly smile.

"We were hoping we'd run into you!" Violet told her cheerfully.

Clarissa gave them a dimpled smile. "Me, too! I wasn't sure how long you'd be staying at the Crooked House."

"Just for a few days," said Jessie. "Mrs. McGregor wanted to see her family home one more time before it's sold. She invited us to come along."

"You can play hockey with us, if you want!" offered Benny. "We only have four sticks, but we can take turns sitting out. We marked the ice where the nets are supposed to be. We don't really have any nets. You have to pretend."

"I've never played hockey before," Clarissa told them. "It sounds like fun, but I just remembered something . . . important I forgot to do. I'd better hurry. Thanks anyway." And with that, Clarissa disappeared behind the trees.

"That's a bit strange, don't you think?"

remarked Violet. "Why would Clarissa change her mind about skating?"

Henry shrugged. "Maybe she just doesn't like hockey."

"I guess it's possible," Violet said slowly, but she didn't sound convinced.

The Aldens finished their hot chocolate, then they grabbed their hockey sticks and stepped back onto the ice. They were soon laughing and shouting as they chased the puck here, there, and everywhere. Henry was the fastest skater. He usually reached the puck first, then passed it smoothly back to the others. When Benny scored a goal, Henry, Jessie, and Violet always cheered loudly for him.

When the Aldens finally trudged back to the Crooked House, they were tired and hungry from their busy morning out-of-doors. It wasn't long, though, before Madeline's chili and Mrs. McGregor's homemade potato chips put them in good spirits again. Nola Rawlings had gone into town for the afternoon, so they all enjoyed a cheerful meal together.

Benny gulped down the last of his milk. "I don't think Nola likes us," he said at last.

"Now, now," said Mrs. McGregor. "How could anyone not like the Aldens?"

"I wouldn't worry, Benny," added Madeline. "Nola isn't very friendly to anyone. I tried asking her a few questions the first time we had dinner together. But she got very uncomfortable. She doesn't seem to like talking about herself."

"Just like the Mystery Lady," observed Henry.

Madeline set another bowl of chili in front of Benny. "I don't care much for mysteries, myself. Never have, never will!" Changing the subject, she said, "I heard you ran into Clarissa today. She stopped in for a while just after seeing you."

Violet was surprised. Didn't Clarissa say she was in a hurry? It was strange that she had time for visiting.

"She's such a sweet girl," Madeline told them. "Clarissa comes here every day after school until Nick gets home from work. We've become very close friends."

"Mrs. McGregor's always there when we get home," Violet said, smiling at their housekeeper.

"If you're looking for a pleasant way to pass the afternoon," Madeline told them as they helped clear the table, "you'll find jigsaw puzzles in the living room cupboard. And we have a wonderful library here at the Crooked House."

"Plenty of books on riddles, too!" added Mrs. McGregor, her eyes twinkling.

When they were washing the dishes, Henry had an idea. "Why don't we look through those books on riddles. Maybe we'll come across one that mentions dragon teeth!"

Benny was excited. "If we find the riddle, then the answer'll be there, too!"

As soon as the dishes had been put away, the Aldens went into the living room to sit by the warm fire. While Violet worked on her sketch of the Crooked House, Henry, Jessie, and Benny browsed through the books of riddles. Jessie helped Benny with some of the harder words. They didn't even hear Mrs. McGregor when she came into the room.

"Ah, what a cozy scene!" Mrs. McGregor smiled. Then she turned to the youngest Alden. "Did you find that mystery book, Benny? The one by Amelia Quigley Adams?"

"Oops!" cried Benny. "I forgot!"

Jessie smiled. "You didn't forget, Benny. You fell asleep by the fire last night. Henry had to carry you up to bed!"

Benny seemed surprised to hear this.

Mrs. McGregor chuckled. "A warm fire on a cold night has that effect on me, too, Benny." Mrs. McGregor went over to the bookcases that lined the far wall. "The whole set of the Amelia Quigley Adams mysteries is right here. Just take your pick!"

Benny hurried over and pointed to the one he wanted. Mrs. McGregor pulled it down from the shelf. "*The Alphabet Mystery* is one of my most prized possessions," she said. "It was signed by the author herself." Mrs. McGregor opened the book and read the inscription out loud. " 'To Margaret, All Best Wishes from Amelia Quigley Adams.' "

"Did you really meet her in person, Mrs. McGregor?" Benny wanted to know.

Mrs. McGregor shook her head. "No, but the Mystery Lady *did* meet her, and she had this book signed for me."

"I'll be extra careful with it," Benny promised.

"I know you will," Mrs. McGregor assured him. Then she reached into the pocket of her knitted sweater and pulled out a photograph. "Oh, by the way, I came across the snapshot of the Mystery Lady when I took the shoe box back up to the attic today."

The Aldens gathered around to take a look. The woman in the photo was sitting on a blanket out-of-doors having a picnic lunch. Her face was hidden under a wide-brimmed hat.

"As I was saying, it's not a great picture,"

Mrs. McGregor went on. "The Mystery Lady would never go anywhere without that big hat to keep her face shaded from the sun."

"It looks bigger than she is!" Benny said.

Mrs. McGregor laughed. "I remember that hat so well! She would always leave it behind so that it would be here for her next visit. And it stayed on that hat tree in the hall for the longest time while we waited for her to return! Finally, though, we packed the hat away in its hatbox and put it up in the attic." Mrs. McGregor tucked the photo back into her pocket. "Nothing stays the same forever, I guess." Then, with a little sigh, Mrs. McGregor hurried out of the room.

"We *must* find that treasure for Mrs. McGregor," said Jessie as they gathered by the fire again.

"I agree," said Henry, and the others nodded.

Violet was squirming in her chair. Something was poking her in the back. When she twisted around, she noticed that a book had slipped behind the cushion. Tugging it out, Violet glanced at it curiously. "Mrs. McGregor must be reading this," she remarked. "It's the published journals of Amelia Quigley Adams."

"What's a journal?" asked Benny.

Jessie said, "It's like a diary. You write your thoughts down in it every day."

Just then, Nola appeared in the doorway. She was still wearing her coat. When she spotted the book on Violet's lap, her face turned a deep shade of red. She rushed over and snatched it away. "How dare you!" Nola sounded upset. "You have no business snooping into things that don't concern you! It's a good thing I came back early."

Violet's eyes widened in alarm. "But I was only — "

The young woman walked away before Violet could finish. At the doorway, Nola turned slowly around and said in an icy voice, "I sincerely hope this never happens again!" And then she was gone.

The Aldens looked at one another in disbelief.

"Why was she so angry?" asked Violet. Her voice shook a little. "I didn't mean any harm."

Jessie got up and put an arm around her sister. "You didn't do anything wrong," she said, trying to comfort her. "Nola wouldn't even give you a chance to explain."

"I didn't know the book was hers," Violet pointed out. "There was a name written inside, but the name was Rebecca Flagg."

"Rebecca Flagg?" echoed Benny.

Henry shrugged. "Maybe Nola borrowed the book from a friend."

Jessie had been thinking. "Didn't Nola say she wasn't interested in Amelia Quigley Adams?"

Violet nodded slowly. "But why would she pretend she wasn't?"

"That's just what I was wondering," said Henry thoughtfully.

The Aldens exchanged glances. They were each thinking the same thing. Maybe the riddle of the dragon's teeth wasn't the only mystery at the Crooked House!

CHAPTER 7

Look Out!

The Aldens had searched through all the books of riddles but found absolutely nothing that would help them. So the next morning, they decided to take a break for a while. After a breakfast of hot oatmeal and blueberry muffins, they bundled up in their warmest clothes and went outside to build a snowman.

As Henry lifted the head onto the snowman's body, Jessie said, "Oh, dear! Our snowman is leaning over to one side!"

Henry stood back to take a look. "He

sure is! Just like the chimney."

"We made a crooked man to go with the Crooked House!" Benny cried out with delight.

The idea made them all laugh. "He does seem to fit right in!" said Henry.

"Hmmm," said Violet thoughtfully. "I think our crooked snowman still needs a little something."

Henry looked around until he found a broken branch on the ground. A few minutes later, Benny came running out of the house with a funny-shaped carrot. Soon their snowman had a crooked walking stick and a crooked nose!

Nick and Clarissa were walking out to their car. They came over to see what all the excitement was about.

"Oh, look!" cried Clarissa. "A crooked snowman!"

Nick threw his head back and laughed. "Now all you need is a crooked cat!"

Benny nodded. "I remember that nursery rhyme! The crooked man bought a crooked cat who caught a crooked mouse."

"And they all lived together in a little crooked house!" everybody sang out at the same time.

"Our snowman leans to the right," Benny told Mrs. McGregor over a lunch of chicken noodle soup and toasted tomato sandwiches. "That means he's a very friendly snowman, doesn't it, Jessie?"

Jessie reached over and ruffled her younger brother's hair. "That's just for handwriting, Benny!"

"Oh, are you children interested in handwriting?" Madeline's eyebrows shot up. "Nick's been studying it for years. Did you know that he can look at someone's handwriting and tell you exactly what sort of person they are? It's really quite amazing."

"Is Nick an expert in handwriting analysis?" Nola sounded surprised.

Jessie and Henry exchanged glances. Why was Nola suddenly so interested in their conversation?

"It's just a hobby of his," said Madeline. "But he's really quite good at it."

"Jessie's good at it, too," Benny put in. "She could tell that Henry was a hard worker and that Violet was helpful just by looking at their handwriting. And Jessie was right! It was Violet's idea to decorate a tree with food for the birds. That was *very* helpful."

Madeline nodded approvingly. "If you'd like to help the birds of Riddle Lake, feel free to use whatever you can find in the kitchen."

"Thank you," said Violet shyly. "We'll make some decorations when we get back from tobogganing."

As they made their way up the snowy slope, Henry said, "Just one more ride down, then we'd better start back."

They had been tobogganing all afternoon. Clarissa had come along, too, and the sun was just starting to set as they piled on for one last ride. Benny was in front, with Clarissa, Violet, and Jessie behind him. "Hold on tight!" hollered Henry. He gave the toboggan a push, then hopped onto the back.

Zooming down the hill, they all shouted and squealed as the snow sprayed back into their faces. About halfway down, the toboggan went off course. Before they knew what was happening, they were heading straight for a tree!

"Look out!" cried Clarissa.

But it was too late. Everybody tumbled into the snow when the toboggan collided into the tree with a great *thunk*!

"Is everyone okay?" asked Henry, shaking the snow from his hat.

For a moment, they were all laughing too hard to speak. Finally, Benny held up an icicle. "Look! We knocked out the tree's tooth."

Everyone laughed at Benny's joke. Then Violet began to stare wide-eyed at the tree.

"What's the matter?" Jessie asked her in alarm.

Scrambling to her feet, Violet rushed over and snapped another icicle from a branch. "It really *does* look like a tooth," she said. "A dragon's tooth!"

When Violet started to recite the riddle

aloud, the other Aldens chimed in. By now, they knew it by heart. When they were finished, Benny cried out, "Wait a minute! A tree loses its teeth when the icicles melt!"

Jessie's eyes were sparkling. "And it gets new teeth when the winter comes around again. Just not the kind of teeth that bite."

"Of course!" agreed Henry. "A tree *does* have bark, so its — "

"Bark is worse than its bite!" finished Violet. "The answer to the riddle is a *tree*!"

The Aldens let out a cheer. Putting together clues was always fun.

"I'm glad you found the answer to the riddle," Clarissa told them as they headed home. "Even if it did take longer than just a second!"

Jessie looked confused. How did Clarissa know about the P.S. at the end of the Mystery Lady's note?

When they were back at the Crooked House, they waved good-bye to Clarissa. As soon as she was out of earshot, Jessie said, "Nobody told Clarissa that it was supposed to take a second to find the treasure. How did she know?"

"Maybe Madeline told her about it," suggested Henry.

"I doubt it," said Jessie as they went around to the back of the house. "Madeline doesn't even believe there *is* a treasure."

Violet thought about this. "Clarissa might have overheard us talking yesterday. Don't forget, she was standing right behind us when we were taking a break from playing hockey."

"I guess that's possible," admitted Jessie. But she wasn't so sure.

Henry put the toboggan away in the shed, then fastened the lock on the door. "Well, at least we found the answer to the riddle!"

Benny seemed worried. "But we still don't know where the treasure is hidden. Do we?"

"I think I know where to look!" Violet said, her voice excited.

When their boots were lined up neatly by

the door and their knitted hats were all hanging on the hat tree, the Aldens raced up the crooked stairs behind Violet. Dashing into the room with the cornflower-blue wallpaper, Violet pointed to the Mystery Lady's painting on the wall.

Everybody stared at it for a moment. Then Jessie said thoughtfully, "There *are* icicles on the trees in that picture. But I doubt the painting's worth very much, Violet. Mrs. McGregor told us that the Mystery Lady was just a beginner."

"That's true," said Violet. "But what if there's something hidden in the back of the frame?"

That was possible. They decided to check. Henry lifted the painting down from the wall. And sure enough, Violet was right! They found a note just under the backing.

"It's another riddle," Henry told them. Then he snapped his fingers. "That's what the Mystery Lady meant! She wasn't talking about time when she said it would take a *second* to find the treasure."

"I don't get it," responded Benny.

"I think I do," said Jessie. "She meant it would take a second *riddle*!"

Henry nodded.

"Well, what does it say, Henry?" Benny asked.

Henry read the riddle out loud:

> " 'Look around and you will see,
> A thing that hangs upon a tree;
> If you're partial to the shade,
> Just keep this thing with you all day!
> What is it?' "

"What does *partial* mean?" asked Benny.

"It means, if you prefer the shade to the sun," explained Violet.

Jessie sighed. "The second riddle is certainly a mystery, too!"

"I just hope it's a mystery we can solve," replied Henry.

CHAPTER 8

A List of Suspects

After hanging the Mystery
Lady's painting on the wall again, the children hurried downstairs to prepare their
dinner of sweet-and-sour meatballs, mashed
potatoes, green beans, and fruit salad. The
Aldens were on their own tonight. Mrs.
McGregor and Madeline were dining with
an old friend, and Nola wouldn't be back
from town until later. Jessie carefully read
the recipe that Madeline had left for them,
so she could help instruct her brothers and
sister with the meal.

While they worked in the kitchen, Henry, Jessie, Violet, and Benny discussed the second riddle.

Benny was shaping the meat into little balls. "I bet the answer is an umbrella!" he said.

"That's a good guess, Benny," said Jessie, stirring the sweet-and-sour sauce at the stove. "An umbrella *does* give shade, but—"

"It doesn't hang on a tree," finished Benny with a sigh. Then his face suddenly brightened. "A possum hangs upside down from a tree!"

"That's true," said Violet, chopping bananas and apples for their fruit salad. "But possums aren't known for their shade."

That didn't stop Benny. "How about a possum holding an umbrella?"

The others burst out laughing. Henry gave Benny a little pat on the back. "Keep trying, Benny!" he said. Then he went over to the stove and dropped the peeled potatoes into a pot of water.

While they were waiting for the meatballs to bake and the potatoes to boil, the Aldens sat around the kitchen table. Jessie read a chapter of *The Alphabet Mystery* aloud while Benny helped Violet and Henry string cranberries and popcorn for the birds.

When Jessie had finished a chapter, she went to check on the meatballs. The sauce was bubbling nicely. She poked a fork into the potatoes. They were ready for mashing.

Violet laughed as she gathered up the cranberry and popcorn strings. "Oh, Benny! I think you ate more popcorn than you put on the string!"

The youngest Alden couldn't help grinning. "Figuring out riddles makes me hungry."

While Henry mashed the potatoes, Jessie kept an eye on the green beans while they steamed. Violet and Benny set the table.

Benny took a break for a moment to take a look at the famous author's inscription in *The Alphabet Mystery*: "To Margaret, All Best Wishes from Amelia Quigley Adams."

"I can tell that Amelia Quigley Adams had a good imagination!" he said at last. "Just like the Mystery Lady."

"How can you tell that, Benny?" asked Jessie, dishing up the meatballs.

"Because of her handwriting," Benny pointed out. "See all her high loops?"

Jessie set the meatballs on the table, then she went over to take a closer look. A frown crossed her face. "How odd! The *t*'s are crossed the same way, too. Why, it looks *exactly* like the Mystery Lady's handwriting."

Violet was pouring milk into the glasses. "Are you sure?" she gasped.

"I can't be certain," admitted Jessie. "But I think so."

"Maybe we should compare the two," suggested Henry.

Jessie nodded. "That's a good idea."

Benny sat down quickly at the table. "Not until we are done eating! We don't want our food to get cold. Do we?"

Henry laughed. "Don't worry, Benny. We're hungry, too!"

"Didn't Mrs. McGregor take the shoe

box back up to the attic?" Violet asked as she passed the green beans.

Jessie nodded. "I'm sure she won't mind if we go up for a minute."

During dinner Benny was unusually quiet. Violet could tell something was troubling him. "What's wrong, Benny?" she asked as she served the fruit salad for dessert.

A frown crossed Benny's round face. "I think Madeline is right. I don't think there *is* a treasure!"

"Why do you say that, Benny?" Henry wanted to know.

"The Mystery Lady fooled Mrs. McGregor," replied Benny. "She signed the book herself. Then she pretended the famous author signed it. That was a mean trick to play on Mrs. McGregor."

"Yes, it was," agreed Violet.

Nobody said much for a while. As they cleared the table, Henry remarked, "I guess the Mystery Lady could have fooled Mrs. McGregor about the treasure, too."

"We can't be *certain* the handwriting is

the same," Jessie reminded them. "Not until we compare the two."

As soon as the dishes were done, Henry took one of the flashlights that hung by the kitchen door. Then they headed up to a second flight of crooked stairs that led to the attic.

"Brrr!" said Violet, rubbing some warmth into her arms. "It's freezing up here."

"And dark, too," added Benny, reaching out for Jessie's hand. "It's a good thing Henry brought the flashlight."

Henry beamed the light over trunks and boxes, stacks of books and magazines, and old lamps and paintings. "Never mind. This won't take long."

Benny was the first to spot the shoe box on top of a steamer trunk in the corner. Henry held the flashlight above the shoe box while Jessie looked for the Mystery Lady's note.

"That's funny," she said. "I can't find it in here."

Violet didn't think it was funny at all.

"Look again, Jessie. I saw Mrs. McGregor put the note in there."

"Aaah-chooo!" The dust was making Benny sneeze.

Violet handed Benny a tissue, while Jessie rummaged through the old mementos one more time.

"There's no doubt about it," Jessie said at last. "The note's gone!"

"I can't believe it!" Violet said a little later as they sat by the fire. Her eyes were wide with worry. "Who could have taken Mrs. McGregor's note?"

Benny had an opinion about this. "A thief. That's who!"

Henry threw another log on the fire. "Someone else must be looking for the hidden treasure, too!"

"That means there really *is* a treasure," Benny said. "And it must be a lot more than just a coin or an old toy. I bet it's Nola Rawlings who's looking for it!"

Violet had been thinking the same thing. She told them, "I had a feeling someone was eavesdropping that first night. It's possible Nola Rawlings heard everything Mrs. McGregor said about the hidden treasure."

"Nola *is* very mysterious," agreed Henry. "But we have no proof that it was her."

"I just know it was!" insisted Benny.

Jessie remembered something. "What if Clarissa overheard us talking by the lake? If she did, then she would have known about the treasure, too."

"Clarissa *did* leave in a big hurry," said Henry. "And Madeline said she stopped in for a visit right after seeing us. She could have taken the note before Mrs. McGregor had a chance to put the shoe box back in the attic."

Violet wasn't too sure about this. "Maybe," she said in a hesitating voice. "That *was* strange that she had time to visit when she was in such a hurry. But why would Clarissa do something so mean?"

Henry shrugged. "She doesn't seem to have a reason."

Jessie reminded them, "We have to look at *every* possibility."

"Maybe we should add someone else to our list of suspects," declared Henry after a moment's thought.

"Like who?" Benny wanted to know.

"Like Madeline."

They were all so surprised by Henry's words, they were speechless.

"Well, she wasn't exactly happy about us looking for the treasure," Henry explained.

Jessie thought about that. "She just doesn't want us to get our hopes up. Don't forget, Madeline doesn't even believe there *is* a treasure."

"Maybe she wants us to *think* there isn't a treasure," argued Henry. "Maybe she's afraid the treasure might be worth enough to save the Crooked House."

Violet looked confused. "I don't understand. Madeline *wants* to save the Crooked House. Doesn't she?"

Henry shrugged. "Maybe not. Mrs. McGregor told us that Madeline wanted to sell the house years ago."

Violet nodded, looking less puzzled. "She wanted to do some traveling. Do you think that's what she *still* wants? Is that what you mean, Henry?"

Henry nodded. "She might have taken the note without realizing that Jessie had made a copy of it."

Benny's eyes grew wide. "This is getting more and more mysterious!" he whispered.

CHAPTER 9

Partners in Crime

"Maybe Mrs. McGregor decided to put the note somewhere else," suggested Violet. "You know, for safekeeping. We can ask when she gets home."

Henry agreed. "I guess we shouldn't suspect people until we're certain it was actually stolen."

"And no matter what," declared Benny, "I'm *not* going to fall asleep by the fire tonight!" This was immediately followed by a huge yawn.

Violet smiled at her younger brother. "I

have an idea. Why don't we all go outside and hang the cranberry and popcorn strings for the birds? The fresh air will keep us awake!"

Benny didn't need to be coaxed. They quickly bundled up and went outside.

"What's the matter, Benny?" asked Jessie, when she heard her younger brother's sigh.

Benny was standing in the middle of the front yard with his hands on his hips. "Our crooked snowman looks lonely out here in the dark."

"I know just the thing!" replied Violet. And she proceeded to tie a string of cranberries around the neck of the snowman.

Benny grinned. "Now he looks as if he doesn't have a care in the world!"

"Our snowman *doesn't* have a care in the world," agreed Henry. "He knows it won't be long before the birds arrive. Then he'll have lots of company."

They were busy looping a string of popcorn around a fir tree when a car pulled into Madeline's driveway.

"I bet that's Mrs. McGregor!" Benny

stepped out from the shadows. Then he quickly jumped back again, shaking his head. "It's Nola Rawlings."

Madeline's houseguest was so unfriendly, the Aldens preferred to keep out of her way. They were surprised when Nola got out of her car and headed straight for the Spencers' house without noticing the children in the shadows behind the fir tree.

"What's she doing?" Benny whispered.

Violet shrugged. "I don't know."

They watched as Nola knocked on the door. The children didn't mean to eavesdrop, but they were standing very close to the Spencers' house. They couldn't help overhearing bits and pieces of the conversation.

Nick looked surprised when he opened the door. "What are *you* doing here?"

Nola didn't answer right away. She was too busy glancing nervously over her shoulder. When she turned to face Nick, her back was to the Aldens. They couldn't make

out what she said. But then Nick nodded and replied, "Sure thing. After all, we *are* partners in crime."

Jessie and Benny looked at each other, horrified.

"Did you hear that?" Benny gasped, forgetting to lower his voice.

Violet put a finger to her lips. But it was too late. Nola had already whirled around. The children stood perfectly still, holding their breath. Then Nick said, "Come on in, Rebecca."

Benny's big eyes got even bigger. Had Nick just referred to Nola as *Rebecca*?

The moment the door closed, Violet grabbed Benny's hand, and the Aldens raced across the yard to the Crooked House.

As they sat by the fire, they discussed everything they'd overheard.

"She's just pretending to be Nola Rawlings!" said Benny. "Her *real* name is Rebecca!"

Violet nodded. "Rebecca Flagg. That was the name on the book I found. The one about Amelia Quigley Adams."

"That means Nick isn't the nice person we thought he was," Jessie said sadly. She could hardly believe that Nick was *anybody's* partner in crime.

Violet was frowning. "What I can't figure out is why Nola — I mean, Rebecca — was reading all about Amelia Quigley Adams."

"And why did she make such a secret of it?" demanded Benny.

Violet said in a quiet voice, "It's the oddest thing."

Henry had been thinking. "Unless . . . "

"Unless what, Henry?" Jessie wanted to know.

It took Henry a few moments to answer. "Unless the Mystery Lady wasn't tricking Mrs. McGregor, after all," he finally said. "Maybe Amelia Quigley Adams really *did* sign that mystery book."

Benny said, "But Jessie said the handwriting was just like the Mystery Lady's!"

"What if it looks the same because — " began Henry.

Jessie's eyes widened as she caught Henry's meaning. She finished her brother's sentence for him. "Because the Mystery Lady was none other than Amelia Quigley Adams herself!"

"You think the famous *author* hid the treasure?" asked Benny in amazement.

Henry nodded. "And I'm almost certain that Rebecca Flagg and Nick Spencer are looking for it, too!"

They all thought Henry might be right. "That *would* explain Rebecca Flagg's interest in Amelia Quigley Adams," admitted Violet.

"But we can't be sure that the Mystery Lady really *was* Amelia Quigley Adams," Benny pointed out.

Henry couldn't argue. "Mrs. McGregor just has the one photograph of the Mystery Lady," he said. "And her face is hidden under that big hat."

Jessie stared at Henry. Then her mouth dropped open.

"What's wrong?" Violet asked her sister.

Jessie spoke up. "A hat gives shade from the sun!"

"And it hangs on a tree," added Violet in surprise. "A hat tree!"

Benny almost shouted with excitement, "Then the answer to the riddle is . . . "

"A *hat*!" the Aldens all cried out at once.

"Of course!" said Henry. "Mrs. McGregor told us that the Mystery Lady never went anywhere without a hat to keep her face shaded from the sun!"

"That's true," observed Jessie. "And remember what else Mrs. McGregor said? Her hat was packed away in its hatbox and taken up to the attic!"

"What are we waiting for?" cried Benny. "Let's go up and take a look!"

So once again, Henry, Jessie, Violet, and Benny climbed the creaky stairs to the cold, dark attic. It took them a while, but they finally found the hatbox tucked away behind a standing mirror. Inside was the same wide-brimmed hat that the Mystery Lady had been wearing in the photo. Except for the hat, though, there was absolutely nothing else in the box.

"I don't get it," said Benny. "An old straw hat isn't much of a treasure!"

"But the riddles have led us right here," Jessie pointed out.

"What do we do now?" asked Violet.

Henry shrugged. "It's a mystery, that's for sure!"

CHAPTER 10

A Hidden Treasure

"There *must* be something else here," said Jessie. "Something we're not seeing."

This got Henry thinking. Reaching into the hatbox, he patted all around. Finally, he pulled up gently on the flowery paper that lined the bottom. "I think there's something here!"

"What is it?" Violet asked in a hushed voice.

Henry lifted the lining away and shone the light into the box. "It looks like a story."

"A very old manuscript," added Jessie. "It's all yellowed with age. Just like the note."

"What's a manuscript?" asked Benny.

"A story that's ready to send to a publisher," explained Jessie.

Henry peered closely at the top page. "This one's called *The Crooked House Mystery*."

"And look!" Violet was glancing over Henry's shoulder. "It says it was written by Amelia Quigley Adams."

"Wow!" cried Benny. "You mean Amelia Quigley Adams wrote a mystery about Mrs. McGregor's family home? But . . . I've never seen *The Crooked House Mystery* in the Greenfield Library."

"Neither have I," said Jessie thoughtfully. "I don't think it was ever published."

The attic stairs suddenly gave a loud creak.

"Who's that?" asked Violet in alarm.

Jessie put a protective arm around Benny as Henry clicked off the flashlight.

"I don't know," whispered Henry. He

peeked out from behind the mirror just as a shadow appeared in the doorway.

The inky outline began to move slowly into the deeper darkness of the attic, with its own beam from a flashlight leading the way.

Benny tried to stay very still and quiet. But the dust was tickling his nose. There was nothing he could do! His nose started to twitch, and then suddenly a sneeze escaped! "*Aaah-chooo!*"

"Who's there?"

It was Rebecca Flagg! The Aldens recognized her voice immediately. Loud thumping and bumping noises began as Rebecca tried to make her way through the maze of boxes and trunks. Then there was a terrible *thud!*

Henry beamed the light to where Rebecca had tripped and fallen.

Concerned, Violet rushed out from behind the mirror. "Are you all right?"

"I am most certainly *not* all right!" Rebecca pulled away when Violet tried to give her a hand. "You scared me half to death! I

should have known the Aldens would be up here. Snooping around as usual."

"We weren't snooping!" Benny said indignantly as Rebecca got slowly to her feet.

Just then, they heard the thundering sounds of someone racing up the stairs. Then Nick was standing in the doorway, with Clarissa at his elbow.

"What's going on in here?" Nick held up a hand to shield his eyes from Henry's flashlight. "I thought the roof was falling in!"

Rebecca mumbled, "Oh, it's just the Aldens playing games."

"Well, it's too cold to be playing up here," declared Nick. "Let's go downstairs where it's warm."

But Henry, Jessie, Violet, and Benny weren't going anywhere without the hatbox. By the time the Aldens finally made their way downstairs, Mrs. McGregor and Madeline had returned.

"What in the world are you doing with that old hatbox, Henry?" asked Mrs. McGregor as she hung up her coat.

Madeline stepped out of her boots. "Nick

told us you were up in that icy attic." She shook her head disapprovingly. "I just hope you don't catch pneumonia!"

"Nick and Clarissa are in the living room with Nola," said Mrs. McGregor. "Why don't we go in and sit by the fire with them?"

Madeline's tone was stern. "And then you can tell us what this is all about!"

When everyone was gathered in the living room a few minutes later, Henry reached into the hatbox, took out the yellowed manuscript, and handed it to Mrs. McGregor. "The hatbox had a false bottom," he explained. "We found something hidden underneath. Something that belongs to you."

Mrs. McGregor stared down at the pages in bewilderment, while Nick looked over her shoulder and let out a low whistle.

Rebecca rushed over. When she saw the manuscript, she drew in a sharp breath. "For years it's been rumored that Amelia Quigley Adams left behind an unpublished manuscript," she said in a hushed voice.

"But nobody's been able to trace its where-abouts. Until now, that is."

Mrs. McGregor looked more confused than ever. "But . . . how did it get into the hatbox?"

"The Mystery Lady!" Benny piped up. "Her real name was Amelia Quigley Adams."

Mrs. McGregor's eyes widened. "The Mystery Lady and Amelia Quigley Adams were the same person?"

"It can't be!" cried Madeline in disbelief.

"It's true," insisted Rebecca.

Madeline narrowed her eyes. "What makes you so sure, Nola?"

"Her name isn't Nola," Henry stated firmly. "It's Rebecca Flagg."

Madeline and Mrs. McGregor both stared at the young woman.

"Is there anything the Aldens *don't* know?" asked Nick in surprise.

"We know a lot," Benny told him. "We even know that you and Rebecca were plan-ning to steal the treasure from Mrs. Mc-Gregor!"

Madeline looked horrified. "Benny, what a terrible thing to say!"

Rebecca dropped into a chair. "It's high time you knew the truth. My real name *is* Rebecca Flagg."

Madeline and Mrs. McGregor were too shocked to speak.

"Please, let me explain," Rebecca went on. "I'm not a thief, and neither is Nick. The fact is, I'm a writer. For the past year, I've been working on a biography of Amelia Quigley Adams. I've been trying to fill in some of the missing gaps in her life. And I've been hoping I just might be able to find her famous missing manuscript at the same time.

"You see, for a few weeks every summer Amelia would vanish into thin air. I suppose it was her way of escaping from the demands of editors and fans. But it's always been a mystery where she went. Then one day, I happened to come across a small sketch. Just something doodled into a corner of Amelia's notepad."

"What was it?" asked Madeline curiously.

"It was a drawing of a house with crooked windows and a crooked door. And a funny crooked chimney."

"Oh!" cried Mrs. McGregor.

Rebecca went on, "I didn't pay much attention to it at first. At least, not until I was invited to a dinner party about a month ago. That's when I heard one of the guests mention his holidays. He said he'd stayed at a Crooked House on Riddle Lake. I could hardly believe my ears!" Rebecca stopped talking and took a deep breath. "I managed to get Madeline's phone number, and I called the very next day. I asked for her permission to poke around the house a bit."

All eyes turned to Madeline.

"I do remember a phone call about a month ago," Madeline said slowly. "Someone inquiring about a guest who supposedly left something behind years ago." Madeline looked at Rebecca. "I thought you were accusing me of keeping something — something that didn't belong to me."

"I was so excited at the time," Rebecca

was forced to admit, "I probably didn't explain myself very well. I ended up offending you, Madeline. I didn't know *what* to do then. That's why I decided to go by a different name: Nola Rawlings."

"That way, you could visit the Crooked House anyway," guessed Henry.

"Yes, and truly I'm sorry for the deception, Madeline," Rebecca apologized. "But I was afraid you wouldn't let me stay if you knew I was the woman who had phoned."

Nick spoke up. "I'm just as much to blame. When I happened to run into Rebecca in town, and she mentioned she was staying at the Crooked House, I told her about your plans to sell the place, Madeline. And that's when she explained her real reason for coming to Riddle Lake. I suggested she keep pretending her name was Nola Rawlings for a while."

"But why?" asked Madeline. "Why would you do such a thing?"

Nick sighed. "Because Rebecca wasn't sure she was on the right track."

"That's right," agreed Rebecca. "I'd been

trying to match other sketches of Amelia's with houses in the neighborhood and with buildings in town. Many places had changed over the years, so I used photographs from the town archives. It wasn't long before I knew that Amelia must have spent a great deal of time at Riddle Lake. I still wasn't sure, though, if she'd actually stayed at the Crooked House."

Nick interrupted. "Since it was just a hunch, I suggested not saying anything to you, Madeline. Not until there was more proof that the Crooked House really had been Amelia's secret getaway. I didn't want you to be disappointed if there was no treasure."

Henry looked at Rebecca. "So you tried to make us think you had no interest in Amelia Quigley Adams."

"That's right," confessed Rebecca. Then she smiled a little. "I must admit, it startled me when Mrs. McGregor asked if I was a fan of Amelia's. I was afraid she knew the truth about me."

Mrs. McGregor had a question. "Why

would the Mystery Lady — I mean, Amelia — hide her manuscript?"

Rebecca frowned. "To make a long story short, Amelia's publishing company was sold. She didn't like the new people who started to work on her books. They wanted Amelia to take a new direction with her books. They thought her books were too gentle and old-fashioned for the market. They were wrong, of course. Those are the very qualities that have made Amelia's books popular throughout the years."

"Poor Amelia!" cried Violet. "What did she do?"

"Well, for one thing," responded Rebecca, "she refused to change a single word. Finally, she decided not to publish her latest manuscript at all."

"Instead, she hid the manuscript away in the hatbox," said Jessie, nodding.

"Yes, and soon after that, she became very ill." Rebecca cleared her throat. "Sadly, Amelia passed away the following winter."

"Oh, dear!" said Mrs. McGregor. "That was always my worst fear."

After a long pause, Rebecca continued. "No one ever found her manuscript, so you can imagine my surprise when I heard about a riddle that would lead to a hidden treasure!"

"You were listening when Mrs. McGregor told us about the Mystery Lady, weren't you?" said Violet.

Rebecca lowered her eyes, and her face reddened. "Yes, I admit I was standing in the hallway."

"Violet had a feeling someone was eavesdropping," said Jessie. "Did you tell Nick and Clarissa everything?"

Rebecca nodded. "I always kept them posted on any new developments."

Jessie turned to Clarissa. "So that's how you knew about the P.S. at the end of the note!"

Clarissa looked over at the Aldens sheepishly. "I couldn't admit that I already knew about the riddle. Not without explaining about Rebecca, too."

Just then Benny turned to Rebecca. "You took the note, didn't you? The one the

Mystery Lady wrote to Mrs. McGregor."

Rebecca hesitated, then she reached into her vest pocket and pulled out the yellowed paper. "I intended to put it back. That's what I was doing up in the attic earlier. I just needed it long enough for Nick to study the handwriting. And from the way he described the person who wrote it, I knew it could be none other than Amelia Quigley Adams. She was the guest known to everyone as the Mystery Lady."

Nick nodded. "We agreed it was time to explain everything to you, Madeline. We were just waiting for you to get home. We were hoping you'd want to make a thorough search of the house when you heard about Amelia's manuscript."

Puzzled, Violet said, "There are some things I don't understand. What did you mean when you said that you and Nola were partners in crime?"

"Oh, you heard that, did you?" Nick was smiling. "It's not what you think. It was just a joke. My only crime was not wanting Madeline to get her hopes up for nothing."

Violet turned to Clarissa. "And why did you rush away so quickly when we invited you to go skating?"

Clarissa looked down at her hands. "I didn't know Madeline had decided for sure to sell the Crooked House. Not until Jessie mentioned it at the lake that day. I was so upset, I had to find out from Madeline if it was true."

"I'm sorry you found out like that." Madeline put her arm around Clarissa. "I should have told you sooner, but I didn't want to spoil your holidays."

Henry was wondering about something. "What will you do with the manuscript, Mrs. McGregor?"

After a few moments, Mrs. McGregor said, "It isn't mine alone, Henry. This manuscript belongs to Amelia's fans everywhere. I'll make sure it gets to the right publisher. Someone who won't change a single word."

Nick was grinning from ear to ear. "The Crooked House will get all the free advertising it needs with the publication of that manuscript! And on top of that, there's the biography that Rebecca is writing. Why, people will soon be coming from every corner of the world to spend time at the Crooked House!"

Madeline wiped away a tear. "I can't believe it! We can keep our family home after all."

Benny looked surprised. "But don't you want to travel?"

"Oh, I like traveling, Benny," replied Madeline. "And I hope one day to be able to do a lot more. But I realized a long time ago that there's no place like home! And I'm sorry I tried to discourage you from searching for the treasure," she added. "I just wanted to spare you the same disappointment my sister had experienced years ago."

Rebecca smiled at the Aldens for the first time. She was a changed person now that the truth was out in the open. "I can't thank you enough for finding the manuscript. And I'm really sorry for being so . . . " Her voice trailed away.

"Unfriendly?" asked Benny.

"Yes, Benny," said Rebecca. "I thought if

I kept my distance, no one would ask me any personal questions."

"Oh," said Violet, beginning to understand.

"Finding the treasure was very important to me," added Rebecca. "And I couldn't help thinking it was a game to the Aldens."

"It wasn't just a game to us!" exclaimed Violet.

"It was more than that," agreed Jessie. "A lot more."

Henry added, "We were trying to help Mrs. McGregor. And we were also trying to—"

"Solve a mystery!" finished Benny.

"I know that now," admitted Rebecca. "I didn't realize the Aldens were such good detectives!"

"They're the very best kind of detectives," declared Mrs. McGregor. "They're the kind who believe in teamwork."

Just then, Jessie leaned over and whispered in Violet's ear. Violet dashed from the room. She returned a few minutes later with her sketch of the Crooked House. As everyone gathered around, she presented it to Mrs. McGregor.

"Oh, Violet!" cried Mrs. McGregor. "I'll treasure this always!"

Madeline sighed happily. "Not even Amelia Quigley Adams could come up with a happier ending to a mystery than this!"

Explore the All-New
BoxcarChildren.com

Visit www.BoxcarChildren.com today, where you can join the fan club, ask the Boxcar Children a question, find out about new books and movies, download free activities, sign up to receive our newsletter, and much more!

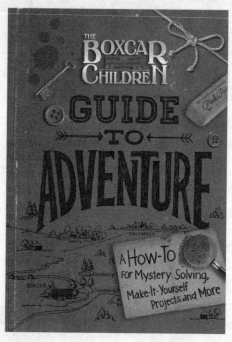

THE BOXCAR CHILDREN®

GREAT ADVENTURE

A Brand-New 5-Book Miniseries

Henry, Jessie, Violet, and Benny Alden are on a secret mission that takes them around the world!

When Violet finds a turtle statue that nobody's seen before in an old trunk at home, the children are on the case! The clue turns out to be an invitation to the Reddimus Society, a secret guild dedicated to returning lost treasures to where they belong.

Now the Aldens must take the statues and seven mysterious boxes across the country to deliver them safely—and keep them out of the hands of the Reddimus Society's enemies. It's just the beginning of the Boxcar Children's most amazing adventure yet!

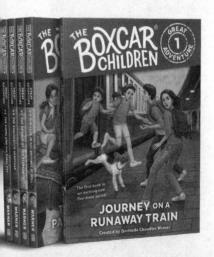

#1: Journey on a Runaway Train
HC 9780807506950, $12.99 · PB 9780807506967, $6.99

#2: The Clue in the Papyrus Scroll
HC 9780807506981, $12.99 · PB 9780807506998, $6.99

#3: The Detour of the Elephants
HC 9780807506844, $12.99 · PB 9780807506851, $6.99

#4: The Shackleton Sabotage
HC 9780807506875, $12.99 · PB 9780807506882, $6.99

#5: The Khipu and the Final Key
HC 9780807506813, $12.99 · PB 9780807506820, $6.99

It's more than just a mystery.

www.boxcarchildren.com

Want to Add to Your Boxcar Children Collection?

Start with the Boxcar Children Bookshelf!
Includes the first twelve books, a bookmark with
complete title checklist, and a poster with activities.

978-0-8075-0855-8 · $59.99

And keep solving mysteries with
new titles in the series added each year!

HC 978-0-8075-0705-6
PB 978-0-8075-0706-3

HC 978-0-8075-0711-7
PB 978-0-8075-0712-4

HC 978-0-8075-0718-6
PB 978-0-8075-0719-3

HC 978-0-8075-0721-6
PB 978-0-8075-0722-3

Hardcover $15.99 · Paperback $5.99

GERTRUDE CHANDLER WARNER discovered when she was teaching that many readers who like an exciting story could find no books that were both easy and fun to read. She decided to try to meet this need, and her first book, *The Boxcar Children*, quickly proved she had succeeded.

Miss Warner drew on her own experiences to write the mystery. As a child she spent hours watching trains go by on the tracks opposite her family home. She often dreamed about what it would be like to set up housekeeping in a caboose or freight car—the situation the Alden children find themselves in.

While the mystery element is central to each of Miss Warner's books, she never thought of them as strictly juvenile mysteries. She liked to stress the Aldens' independence and resourcefulness and their solid New England devotion to using up and making do. The Aldens go about most of their adventures with as little adult supervision as possible—something else that delights young readers.

Miss Warner lived in Putnam, Connecticut, until her death in 1979. During her lifetime, she received hundreds of letters from girls and boys telling her how much they liked her books.